THE

FIRFLAKE

A Christmas Story

Anthony R. Cardno

THE

FIRFLAKE

A Christmas Story

Ottawa, KS

ISBN-13: 978-1-62225-7874

First Boralis Books Edition: November 2021
Printed in the United States of America

10 9 8 7 6 5 4 3 2 1

*Interior Design/Layout by Guy Anthony
De Marco, PublicationEngineering.com
Illustrations by Don Cornue
Cover Art & Design by Audra Redington
Editorial Oversight by Bryan Thomas Schmidt*

Dedication

For Mom and Dad,
who taught me how to believe.
and for Buddy and Squirmy Worm,
who reminded me how when I'd forgotten.

'Tis The Season

The first snowflake of the season
Hurries my heart and brightens my eyes
Every year at this time.

From the far north that cloud blows down
Into the open arms of a new year.
Reindeer and snowmen and drummer boys
Fall in place with stars, menorahs and yule logs,
Launching our spirits high
As that first snowflake dances and cavorts with
Kris Kringle, Sinter Klass, Jack Frost, and
Every incarnation of the spirit of the season:

May the light and warmth of the season bring you
Love, Hope, Peace and Prosperity.

MERRY CHRISTMAS,
HAPPY HANUKKAH,
AND A JOYOUS NEW YEAR!

Chapter One

Papa Knecht was awake long before the last starlight of the night dwindled, before the waning low moon settled comfortably behind the ridge, before the dark turned gray and his eyes had to make the instinctual transition from night vision to day. But still he stayed abed, next to Mama Alvarie breathing slowly, until the tip of the sun appeared over the eastern ridge of their valley.

Then Papa rose from his bed. He gently laid aside the great down blankets so as not to disturb

Mama, who had at least an hour yet to sleep before beginning the day's cooking. He slid his feet into warm wool slippers and lifted his eyeglasses off of the end table. The thick wooden bedchamber door offered its usual slight groan at being opened, but this morning (unlike so many others) Mama didn't even roll over in her sleep at the sound. The door slid back into place and Papa Knecht stood alone in the Great Room.

The large stone fireplace looked cool, but some of the coals were still hot; Papa had little trouble building the fire up so that it would be ready for Mama to cook on. On the hearth, one last, thin, metal, spouted pot of cider still held some warmth. Papa poured himself a flagon, pulled his pipe and tobacco off the mantle, and went out onto the front porch to capture the rest of the sunrise. The grandchildren would want a full description later.

He expected to be the only one awake for some time. The storytelling had gone late into the night, Kristoff and Papa Knecht's other sons (by birth and by marriage) telling fanciful tales of times long past and places that never were, ascribing great and legendary deeds to ancestors of the

Ruprecht clan, until the grandchildren either started to fidget or fall asleep and the women took them home. Then the men reminisced about previous winters in anticipation of the day to come. None of them would awaken early.

Papa had just finished lighting his deep-bowled, long-stemmed pipe and had taken his first long satisfying draw of the day when a quick darting movement pulled his eye past the tobacco's lazy smoke curls and out to the frosted grass in front of the house.

A small gray form bounded from the roots of a tall, ancient, thick-bodied tree to a small shrub, and then from the shrub directly for the low wall of the porch. The sound of scrabbling and slipping accompanied a slightly outraged squeak, before a tiny gray head popped over the top railing. A plump body, four small legs, and a bushy, twitching tail followed.

"Well, good morning, Skitch," Papa Knecht smiled, reaching into the small straw sack tied with a corded drawstring to the arm of the chair. He rustled a bit, and then pulled out two chestnuts, offering them on a flat palm to the squirrel. Skitch investigated both, took the one more to his liking, and chattered his thanks.

"You're welcome," Papa Knecht nodded. "Send Squeala by in a few hours, as Mama Alvarie's sure to have breakfast leftovers for you." Skitch chittered again, and Papa added, "Yes, we all think today's the day. Kristoff has only been wrong once, and that was ... well, too long a time ago to think on. But nothing can happen until our Watcher awakens."

Skitch's voice rose and he gestured excitedly, almost dropping the chestnuts.

"Is she now?" Papa squinted into the stand of trees nearest the house. "Squeala saw her where?" More chittering. "The brook? Harrumph. No, I'm not surprised. It's her first year as Watcher; no wonder she's excited. And she's always taken her chores seriously. Still, she's likely to have a long day. Kristoff may be talented at predicting the day, but no one can predict the moment. Thank you, Skitch."

Skitch nodded, too busy tucking the chestnut into his cheeks to respond. When he was done, he bounded off for home. Papa Knecht watched until Skitch disappeared behind a rock, then he set down his flagon and pipe, went inside, and dressed quietly. When he returned to the porch, he untied the chestnut sack from the chair and reattached it to his belt, re-lit his pipe, picked up the flagon and walked unhurriedly across the field, frost crunching under his deer-hide boots. He reached the nearest stand of tall evergreens and paused for a sip of cider. He listened attentively to the sounds of the woods: a few birds chirped, a squirrel (not Skitch, but perhaps a relative) vocalized in a way that sounded indignant to Papa Knecht's ears, and nearby, one little girl hummed.

Papa Knecht smiled. He had taught her the tune when she was just a babe, and it remained her favorite.

Papa Knecht found his youngest granddaughter sitting cross-legged on a flat rock overlooking the brook. For just a moment he fondly absorbed the sight of his "bright angel" (the meaning of her name): her head was cocked at such a severe angle that he knew immediately she was staring intently at the sky, humming through pursed lips. She probably had one eyebrow raised as if to ask the sky what it was waiting for.

"A scolded sky never releases the Firflake, Engleberta," Papa Knecht said kindly. He remained at the tree line. Engleberta was so intent, he could have strolled up and sat beside her before she took notice of him, and then been so startled she'd fall into the stream, which was just short of frozen.

"Papa!" Engleberta ran to him. "Good morning, Papa! Isn't it a glorious morning, Papa? It would be even more glorious if the Firflake would appear." This last was said meaningfully, with a scowl for the cloudless sky above.

"Patience, child." Papa patted her head and offered a small handful of chestnuts – after all, breakfast had not yet been eaten. Papa suspected Engleberta had snuck out before sunrise without a bite to eat; no danger here of a small handful ruining the child's appetite. "No need to rush the event. It will happen when it happens."

"But what if I don't see it?" Engleberta huffed. "What if I'm in the kitchen with Mama Alvarie and the Firflake falls by the old hollow tree?"

"You worry entirely too much." Papa drew on his pipe. "You've not even eaten breakfast, and your stomach is already in knots. Come back to the house and sit with me until Mama needs help cooking."

"Then what?" Engleberta asked, casting another

sullen glance at the sky.

"Then you eat breakfast, and play with your sisters and cousins."

"But...."

"No 'buts'—trust your instincts. You will see the Firflake fall."

Chapter Two

Breakfast passed. Lunchtime arrived and Engleberta finally began to relax, actually allowing herself to look down and around rather than up. She began to play, and by the time Papa Knecht finished cleaning up after the meal and joined Mama Alvarie on the porch, it seemed as though Engleberta had forgotten all about being the Watcher.

As the early afternoon progressed, Kristoff and his wife Katherine and the other adults of the clan slowly and quietly disappeared from the field, walking off into the woods or slipping around the corner of a house when the children weren't watching. It was another tradition of the day, the adults leaving to wrap gifts and cook food in preparation for the night's festivities while Papa and Mama watched over the army of grandchildren. The older children played along, pretending not to notice the sudden absences, going so far as to distract the littler ones while offering the adults a winking signal to vanish. Georg and Wilhelm and Kurt, Kristoff's triplets and the oldest of the grandchildren (only a year away from becoming adults themselves), magically became the center of a huge pile of bodies, or found themselves being chased into the trees by a screaming, giggling horde.

Even Papa Knecht found himself distracted by these games, until he became aware that only one adult remained, lingering near the field. Nanhe was Papa and Mama's youngest son, barely a year into adulthood himself. As the youngest adult, Nanhe had a particular job today, and he looked unready for it. As the children chased Kurt into the trees for a fourth time, Papa motioned for Nanhe to join them on the porch.

"Have some hot cider, Nanhe." Mama Alvarie pushed a flagon at him. "You look cold."

"He looks nervous," Papa laughed. Nanhe blushed. "So. I'm correct."

"Yes, Papa." Nanhe's voice was strained enough to crack. He caught sight of Engleberta, suddenly giving up on the chase and grimacing at the sky. "Was I so intent when I was the Watcher?"

Papa and Mama exploded in deep, rich laughter, a sound that always caught the children's attention. They began to run for the porch. Mama caught her breath and reminded Nanhe of what he had clearly forgotten in the intervening years.

"Your first year as Watcher you sat here on the porch for seventeen hours, eyes fixed on the sky as if you could will the Firflake down. You barely slept the night before and practically refused to eat. Intent is a mild word."

"What happened, Papa? What's so funny?" The children's voices bubbled as they poured onto the porch, little Maria launching herself into Papa's lap while young Loek, last year's Watcher and barely a year older than Engleberta, settled comfortably at Mama's knees, taking up the skein of wool with which she was knitting. Maria took the whittling stick Papa was working on and appraised the handiwork with a smile.

Engleberta herself sat at Papa's feet, where she could see across the field. Nanhe smiled and winked, and she returned the wink.

"Hello, Uncle Nanhe," Kurt bellowed heartily as he ascended the steps to the porch.

"Missed you on the field, Uncle Nanhe," Georg added, slapping Nanhe on the back. They were both doing their most obvious to bring the children's attention to him. Nanhe squirmed slightly.

"Uncle Nanhe," Wilhelm smiled knowingly, "Tell us the story of the Firflake."

Nanhe's eyes widened slightly, although no one noticed except Papa, Mama and the triplets. He had been expecting a little more time to prepare for his debut as Storyteller, and yet here it was, time to begin.

"Yes, tell the story!" the other children clamored and clapped. And Wilhelm beamed at having done his part for the day: instigating the first of the stories.

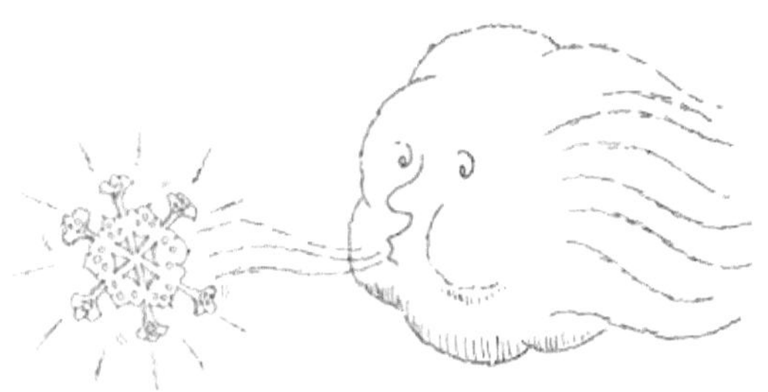

Chapter Three

Nanhe sipped his hot cider then cleared his throat. His voice quavered only slightly as he started the story, becoming accustomed to the cadences and intonations passed down to him from many years of hearing his older siblings tell the tale.

"Well, my little ones. The Firflake is, of course, the very first snowflake of winter – a very important snowflake because its arrival is our signal that not only has winter arrived, but Christmas is not far away, and we have a great deal to do to prepare." He paused while the children murmured agreement at this proclamation. Papa Knecht nodded slightly. "But where does the Firflake come from? Ah, there's the mystery. Yes, indeed." Nanhe smiled slightly, more in his eyes than his lips. His voice was picking up inflection, and with it, the children's rapt attention.

"We live very much at the top of the world here in our valley, and we've grown strong living off of this land and doing the work that we do. But there are lands farther north, frigid ice-locked lands where we could not survive. And this...this is where the Firflake is born.

"Deep in the center of that ice-covered ocean is the birthplace of snow. Like us, no two snowflakes are exactly the same. Each flake is unique, with its own personality and beauty. Like us, any flake stands an equal chance of being chosen for something special. Each year, one is chosen as the Firflake.

"All year long, the clouds create the snow that falls on the icy plains and small ridges. Those snowflakes are charmed never to melt, because the top of the world is an awesomely cold place that protects its own. Those snowflakes never leave their home. By staying in one place, they are secure that no ill ever comes to them.

"But there comes a day each year when all the clouds stop making snow—except for the oldest and wisest cloud. At the proper moment, that cloud creates a single, beautiful, unique snowflake, and the winds blow up strong in celebration. The winds keep that snowflake, the Firflake, aloft, floating just ahead of the cloud that created it. And the fields of snow leap up and whoosh and dance 'fare well' to the first snowflake of the year to leave home and risk a different destiny. The winds push the Firflake and the cloud away from the top of the world, slowly and proudly. They travel over a great distance, with the other clouds following in regal procession. Until they reach us.

"When the Firflake and the company of clouds reach our valley, the winds draw back in a respectful silence. The Firflake catches our cold winter sun as it begins to fall from the sky, and shines a signal to the one watching below."

Nanhe smiled down at Engleberta, who had stopped looking at the sky. Realizing he was speaking of her, she straightened her back against Papa's legs and a blush came to her face. Without a word, she returned her eyes to the blue sky above.

"When the Watcher sees the Firflake falling, she will bring Papa Knecht to stand under it. And Papa will greet the Firflake and welcome it to our home. And we will celebrate the start of the Christmas season."

"Hurrah!" Wilhelm cheered. "Hurrah for Christmas and the Firflake! Hurrah for Uncle Nanhe!" And all the children took up the cheer.

"But wait!" Kurt interrupted. The children gasped and some of the younger ones whispered with concern. When they quieted down, Kurt turned teasingly daring eyes towards Nanhe. "He can tell us where the Firflake comes from, but can he tell us how it was named?" Kurt's lips twitched as he fought back a laugh. Issuing the challenge was part of the tradition. Nanhe rose to it without a pause.

"That's a much shorter tale to tell," he smiled. "When my eldest brother Kristoff—who is father to some of you and uncle to most—saw his first First Snowflake, he was younger than Engleberta is now, and was not quite a good talker yet. So instead of saying, 'Papa, there's the First Snowflake,' Kristoff said, 'Papa, Firflake! Firflake!'

and dragged Papa Knecht to see it. And that is how the Firflake got its name and how our tradition started, almost three hundred years ago." Nanhe paused, a look of mock worry crossing his eyes. "But don't tell Kristoff that I told you how old he is!"

The children broke out in laughter and Nanhe turned appreciative eyes toward Mama Alvarie; he had auditioned the joke about Kristoff's age for her yesterday and gained her approval. Her eyes twinkled at him; Nanhe had been more worried than he needed to be. He was a natural, if somewhat shy, storyteller.

The laughter slowly dwindled, and the children began to talk quietly with each other. Maria handed Papa Knecht his whittling stick, her inspection completed. Loek rotated the skein of dyed wool in his small hands, watching the strands pull loose and rise to Mama Alvarie's knitting needles. For a few peaceful seconds, there was no sound but the light voices of the children, the clicking of Mama's needles and the thin slice of Papa's whittling knife on wood.

"Papa," Loek finally whispered, turning his head ever so slightly in Papa's direction so as not to forget the wool, "Tell us how you met Nicholas."

At once the children's voices rose and rang off the porch-boards: "Yes, another story!" "Yes, Papa!" "Oh, yes, the Nicholas story!"

Papa wordlessly readjusted Maria's position on his lap, took a large sip of cider from the flagon beside his chair, and resumed whittling, all the while patiently waiting for the voices to dwindle first to whispers, then to a few giggles, then to silence.

And only then did he begin.

Chapter Four

ow I met Nicholas..." he began. "Hurm. It was a long time ago indeed. I was a young one myself, barely an adult—just about your Uncle Nanhe's age. Our people were much fewer then, and lived in a land much greener than this.

"I was a restless one, though—couldn't stand to be tied down to hearth and home. So I went to see what the people of the outside world looked like. I was warned that I'd get a cold reception. Because our people are so much shorter than most, and because we have a tendency to keep to ourselves, to our own valleys and hillocks and lands, we're often forgotten by the other people, the taller ones. Or we are turned into fanciful creatures from stories and given magical abilities or strange deformities like knobs on our heads or wings on our backs or cloven hooves.

"I was advised to travel mainly by night, and to stay well hidden during the day, for superstition and fear can be powerful enemies. If I had to make contact with any tall ones, I should do so carefully and try to say as little as possible about myself.

"I traveled for a year this way, and saw many, many interesting sights and people—all stories for another time. Finally, in the deep heart of the winter, long after the first snows had fallen, I came to a town called Ockholm. The snow was deep and the air bitter cold on this night, but the stars shone bright in the black clear sky. The small town, though ... Oh! What warmth! What friendship! In all the houses, candles flickered in the windows, people shared mead and food and fire and song. I had already come upon a comfortable barn in which to rest from the cold wind, thinking I could hide in a dark corner during the day to follow. But

I found myself drawn to the town; I simply could not resist watching the feasting.

"One house in particular drew my attention. It seemed two families had gathered together for an extra special celebration. All within were dressed in the finest of clothing and a large feast was laid on the table. There were two older gentlemen, standing by the fireplace and laughing heartily between drinks. Two older ladies sat together near the hearth and smiled politely, never taking their eyes from the true focus of the gathering: three handsome young men dancing with three beautiful young women, all of them barely adults as the tall ones reckon it. "I was caught up in the happiness and camaraderie of the household, the sense of life cherished and enjoyed, and I wished nothing more than to join them and share in it.

"I stood there staring, going unnoticed by those within, and forgetting where I was for a time, until a sound drew my attention from the window: a scuffling of feet.

"Three harsh-looking boys had spied me in the shadows and had realized that, despite their young age, I was smaller than all and so an easy target for some youthful roughhousing. The tallest of the three whispered something to the others; one of them stooped and snatched up a rock. I remained very still while he hefted the rock twice in the air, and almost didn't notice when the same rock left his hand and flew towards me.

"I realized later that if I had not moved, the rock would have sailed past me and smacked against the house, and possibly brought help. But I panicked and moved into the rock's path—just slightly, enough for the rock to cut the top of my head and draw blood.

"'Hey,' the tallest one called in a half-whisper, 'you should be home in bed.' They thought I was a local boy, someone to pick on. They thought the rock would make me less eager to resist them. With the cut on my head throbbing, I ran back to the edge of town.

"They, of course, knew the town better than I, and were able to cut off my flight. They quickly surrounded me in the shadow of a quiet smith's shop. They began to push me between them, saying, 'Little ones should not be out so late,' and such. One of them pushed me out of the shadows and into a streak of moonlight. Now they could see me clearly and they realized they were not picking on a younger villager.

"'Elf! Dwarf! Gnome! Troll!' Fearful hate replaced mischief in their eyes. One called me a creature of the devil. The second pulled a piece of metal piping from the shop's outdoor pile, telling the others that our people are powerless against cold iron.

"The truth of course is that cold iron will hurt anyone if it hits hard enough. And so it did. They swung the pipe at me, bashing at my hands and ankles and knees, trying to hit my head and chest, but missing in their fear. I realized that they wanted to kill me, but some deeper superstition initially kept them at arm's length as well; the more blows they successfully landed, the closer they moved.

"One eye was already bruised shut when I saw a shadow rise up, and I thought, 'Now they have help.'

"'You!' one of the boys gasped, his voice losing its strength. 'We, ah ....'

"'Go now!' the voice commanded, and the boys ran, forgetting even to drop the pipe. I looked up to see a tall, thin man with a white beard longer than my body, seated on a white horse skittering in the snow. There was a large sack tied behind him, but he seemed unconcerned about anything except me. His face almost radiated warmth as he asked if I was all right. I tried to rise and answer but fell back instead.

"In a trice, he was off the horse and scooping me out of the snow. Dazed as I was, I had no way to tell where he was carrying me, until he burst through the door of a well-lit, cheerful home.

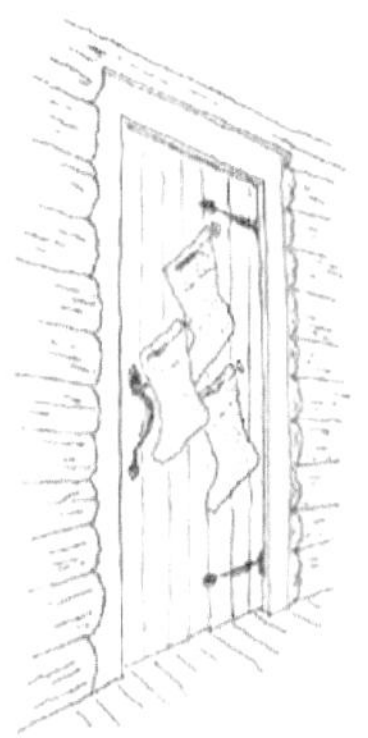

Chapter Five

Papa Knecht paused. He passed his whittling stick gently into Maria's hands and stuck his knife firmly into the arm of his chair. Then he reached down for his flagon and, bringing it to his lips, took a long, satisfying drink. All of this was done with no sense of gravity or ceremony, and yet all of the children's eyes were on him, even Engleberta's. Not a pair was anything but wide. After a moment, Papa set the flagon back on the porch-boards, and Maria handed him back the whittling stick. He resumed whittling and resumed the story as though he had never paused.

"Not a single voice raised in protest or even surprise. They simply set to work bandaging my wounds and warming my body. They kept me warm and fed for days. While I slept, Nicholas left and returned frequently.

"I insisted on doing something to repay their kindness once I was well. As the days went by, I helped by chopping wood, cleaning, and mucking the horse stalls. They tried to get me to do less, but I wanted to earn my keep. They had made me welcome, and had never asked for more personal information than what I was willing to tell in front of the hearth each night. I gave them tales of my travels and in return they explained why Nicholas was so important to them: he had rescued the three sons from drowning when their sleigh cracked through the ice of a nearby frozen lake, and he had provided the girls' family with money to survive that same harsh winter.

"Nicholas came to me one afternoon while I was splitting wood. He took up an ax and worked beside me. I was struck by how old he looked in the bright winter sunlight, and yet how energetic he was.

"'You're a good man, Nicholas,' I said after a while. 'Not many would rescue one of my people, for fear of touching magic.'

"'I am not a superstitious man,' Nicholas replied. 'There are people who would say I am magic myself. The three young men of this family, I saved from drowning. There are rumors in villages miles from here which say I raised them from the dead.'

"'Did you?' I asked.

"'I know no man short of the Son of God who could, and I am not He.' He paused, exhaling a cloud with every thought-filled breath. 'Your people's magic is that they hide well, and know how to travel quicker than we, and that you live longer. You are different from us in only the subtlest of ways. I don't always understand your people, but I accept you. These are hard times, and people fear what is different. So they exaggerate the subtleties and suddenly your people have horns or wings, or serve a darker god. I know better. We are all of us God's creatures, and loved by Him.' And then, Nicholas sighed heavily.

"'What can I do to repay you?' I asked. 'What help do you need?' Again, Nicholas exhaled deeply, and watched the frost from his breath drift skyward.

"'There's something I do on the night of the Christ-child's birth. I deliver gifts on my horse, to the children who have behaved well during the year in the surrounding towns. But it is not easy to do on my own. My wife Karina helps me to prepare the gifts, and then stays home and cooks. But I'm slowing down. I could use an assistant.'

"'Done,' I agreed. 'Come Christmas Eve for me. I'll be ready.'

"A week later, I bid farewell to the families who had been so kind. The young men shook my hand strongly; the ladies kissed me on the cheek. All offered a warm bed and meal whenever I needed one. Later that year, all three couples married.

"But that night...that night, Nicholas led me to a small saddled pony, pawing the snow next to his own white steed.

"'You know Courser,' he said as he patted his horse's strong neck. 'You will be riding Dominic.' I ruffed my hand through Dominic's chestnut mane.

Each mount had a bulging sack of simply wrapped gifts. We set off at a canter, stopping at every house in the village that had stockings hanging near the door. Nicholas would climb down and place gifts in each stocking. He explained that the children had started this so that he would not forget where they lived.

"Near the end of our circuit of the village, we came to two houses close together. The first has a single stocking at the door, the next had two stockings. We stopped our horses, but Nicholas remained in his saddle.

"'What's wrong?' I asked.

"'These are the homes of the boys who injured you.' His voice was heavy with sadness. 'I have no gifts for any person who can do such violence. They owe you a debt. Do what you will.'

"I slid off of the pony, taking only the switch I had been using to gently motivate it. I walked to the first door. During my recuperation, I had thought of the boys often but had not seen them again. Now I had the opportunity. I stood at that door for a long time. Then I looked down and saw a pile of dark rocks covered in soot from the house's chimney. I laid the switch down before I hefted three good-sized rocks and dropped one into each stocking.

"Turning, I smiled at Nicholas.

"We had other towns to visit, and the night was moving on around us. I did something I never expected to do; I shared our magic with Nicholas and taught him how to travel faster. We visited more homes that night and finished earlier than he ever had before. His wife fed both of us well when we returned.

"The next day, the rumors reached us. Nicholas was surely a saint, his far travel was surely a miracle. His companion was a bitter little dwarf who left coal in the stockings of bad children and switched them in their sleep. It was only then that we realized I had left the switch at the boys' home. Dominic, once accustomed to me, had needed no further motivation that night. Nicholas, Karina, and I all laughed.

"'Where will you go now, Knecht?' Karina asked.

"'I'll travel more,' I answered, 'but I'll be back here next Christmas. Nicholas will have many more houses to visit. He'll need help.'

"'Very true.' Nicholas laughed deeply. 'Next year, then. And don't forget the coal.'"

Chapter Six

Mama Alvarie continued to knit, and Papa Knecht continued to whittle. The drawn-out shhhk-shhhk of Papa's knife peeling off wood shavings fell into perfect rhythm with the sharp ki-klick-ki-clack of Mama's needles pulling wool together. Their hands worked at the same speed despite the difference in their tasks. The children sat in silence, knowing that Papa and Mama would finish at the same time, not a moment too soon or too late. It was as much a part of the day's traditions as was the asking of questions and the telling of stories.

Maria fidgeted in Papa's lap; she felt as though she had forgotten something important, something to do with the story. Then she froze, worried that her movements would throw off Papa's whittling. Watching his knife move about the wood in his hand, her eyes widened. She realized that everyone was waiting for the next question to be asked, and they were waiting for her to ask it.

"Papa! What about the team?" Maria blurted the question out quickly. "Every year there were more towns! Your pony and Nicholas' horse couldn't carry all those gifts on their backs!" Maria closed her mouth as quickly as the words were out of it, hoping that she had not ruined the story by waiting so long to ask the question. The other children watched Papa and waited for him to begin again. He spared a slight wink for Maria's eyes only, to make sure she knew that she had done well. Maria smiled shyly in return.

"I left Nicholas' home and resumed wandering. True to my word, I returned to Nicholas' cottage several weeks before Christmas every year. He and Karina would always greet me at the door. They knew, somehow, that I was due to arrive even though I sent no advance notice. It was one of Nicholas' particular talents, like knowing which children deserved gifts and which didn't each year. And every year on Christmas Eve, we would ride out, he on Courser and me on Dominic, with larger and larger sacks of gifts for children in towns wider and wider apart.

"I'd lost track of how many winters it had been since we'd met. One year, Karina alone greeted me at the door. She hugged me and directed me almost immediately to the barn. She spoke only words of happiness, but her eyes showed concern.

"Nicholas was bent over at one of the horse stalls, murmuring softly to whatever animal was within. His posture was troubled, but the tone of his voice was calm and soothing.

"'Nicholas?' I spoke his name softly, so as not to spook the animal to which Nicholas was tending. His head came up only slightly, enough for him to see me out of the corner of his eye.

"'See here, Courser, an old friend has come to check on you.' Nicholas stood and moved slightly to the side so I could see into the open stall.

Courser, that faithful horse which Nicholas had been riding when he'd rescued me from the boys, that powerful horse which had carried so many presents to so many eager children, looked back at me with eyes old and wise. He nickered a greeting and his breath sent the hay around him fluttering. I moved to him, knelt down, and drew my hand gently down his neck. I moved my hand back up, and then down his head toward his nose. He licked my palm when it was close enough to his mouth, and I knew he recognized me.

"'Rest now, Courser.' With a last pat on his head, I stood. We walked back towards the house, with Nicholas stopping only to make sure the door was closed fast. There were wolves in the area who might take notice of an old horse.

"'It won't be long now,' Nicholas told Karina as we entered. She had cups of steaming hot cider ready and her hand shook slightly as she passed them to us. Nicholas turned to me. 'He's been eating less and less throughout the year. I had hoped he'd improve, but he's been off his feed for two weeks, and in the past two days he's not eaten a thing. But he's held on, almost as though he was waiting to see you.'

"'Oh, Nicholas,' Karina spoke so softly we barely heard her. 'How will you deliver the gifts? Dominic is too small even if he was young and strong, and we can not afford to buy another horse.'

"At that moment, movement on the snow caught my eye. I stared through the frosty glass, trying to focus through the darkness outside the house. Clouds parted for a moment, and stronger moonlight glinted off of the ice-covered antlers of a majestic reindeer standing just before the tree line. I rose from my seat suddenly, startling Nicholas and Karina.

"'I have an idea, Nicholas. Give me but a moment.' I went outside. Even at the opening of the door, the buck stood still on the rise. I whistled softly to it, and it turned to look at me.

"'We need your help,' I told him as I approached. 'Your kind have the gift of travel, as my own people do. I have shared that knowledge with this man, to help with the good work he does. His horse is ill. Will you help us?'

"The reindeer nodded once at me, his large antlers dipping low, almost to the snow. Then he bounded off into the trees. I knew he would be back. Nicholas and Karina had appeared in the doorway while I'd been speaking to the reindeer.

"'Full of surprises, even after all these years,' Nicholas smiled. 'Thank you, Knecht.'

"Not an hour later, there was a clamor that drew our attention. We three went to the door and out. Eight adult reindeer stood on the rise: four proud males and four beautiful females. They were with a group of young who were waiting farther in the trees. They all bowed their heads at us. Nicholas and I bowed from the waist in return, and Karina dropped her deepest curtsy.

"'These are your coursers now,' I told Nicholas. 'The lead male is Dasher, his female is Dancer. Then Prancer and Vixen, Comet and Cupid, Donder and Blitzen. These eight will replace the one who has worked so hard, and will do his memory proud.'

"Later that night, we all gathered in the barn. Nicholas cradled his horse's head in his lap, and Karina stroked his neck. Dominic rubbed his ears against my waist and whinnied softly. The reindeer stood behind us, their heads bowed in respect for the noble creature before them. And so Courser left us, in peace and surrounded by love.

Chapter Seven

ventually, I found a clan of our people, met a beautiful lady of my own, and we married. That Christmas, Mama Alvarie and I both helped Nicholas and Karina, as we have every year since.

"His people were right about one thing: Nicholas surely is a saint, because of what he is inside—a good person. And because of that, he was granted a life longer than any since Biblical times."

Papa Knecht stopped talking, and with a smile,

held up his whittling stick. The sun, only a hand or so above the western ridge, caught the completed figure: a tall thin man with a long beard, holding a sack over his shoulder. The children "oohed" and "ahhed."

"I'll put it on the mantle," Mama Alvarie fussed, rising from her seat and handing Loek her knitting needles to hold. In one hand she held the long woolen scarf she had finished as Papa had finished his figure. She took the figure from Papa and turned towards the front door. A loud and unexpected chatter made her pause.

Skitch and Squeala and their five young were scrambling onto the porch railing. The children were up in a flurry, gathering around the squirrels and talking to them. One of the youngest squirrels jumped on Loek's shoulder and playfully batted his ear. Loek giggled. Skitch and Squeala each offered an acorn to Papa Knecht and Mama Alvarie. The children played and jostled and Mama poured a bowl of water for the squirrels while Papa refilled the cider flagons for himself, Mama and Nanhe.

The sun was touching the western ridge, ready to set, when Engleberta's voice rang out.

"Papa! Papa! The Firflake!" she called. All of

the children began to look around excitedly, but Engleberta was nowhere nearby. "Over here!"

Papa took Mama's hand and led her toward the stand of trees, where Engleberta stood waving frantically. Nanhe and the children and the squirrels all followed.

"I was right, Papa!" Engleberta beamed. "Come to the brook." She took his hand and led her grandparents to the brook's edge. Then she respectfully stepped back.

Papa looked up to the white dot slowly drifting in beautiful zigs and zags toward him.

"Hello, little one," he smiled in greeting. "Hello, Firflake. Welcome to our valley. May you be the first of many."

Papa Knecht held his hands out in a bowl shape, and as the Firflake settled between them, he breathed gently on it. The Firflake glowed. It grew, stretching in all directions until it filled the space between Papa's hands. Then it froze solid.

"Kristoff will put the Firflake at the top of our tallest tree," Papa Knecht announced. The children began to cheer. Loek jumped into his Uncle Nanhe's arms, the youngest squirrel leaping from Loek's shoulder to a nearby branch. All of the squirrels' voices rose joyously.

A deep, rich laugh resounded through the trees. A figure appeared behind Nanhe, a man still tall, if no longer thin, with a long white beard. He laughed and hugged the beautiful, robust woman with him. Behind him, roaming through the trees and grazing, were families of reindeer.

"Nicholas!" Maria cheered, leaping to his arms.

"Happy Holidays, children!" Nicholas bellowed. "Nanhe. Our son has been asking for you since we arrived. He's in the Great Room."

"Nathaniel is here?" Nanhe asked. "On my way!" He set Loek down and hurried into the trees. Mama Alvarie hugged Karina and called, "Children! Let's go to the field. Your parents are waiting."

As the hoard of children began to skitter through the woods, jostling and laughing, Papa Knecht cleared his throat. It wasn't a loud or commanding noise, but it got the attention it needed. Loek, halfway to the treeline, turned back.

"Papa?"

"Forgetting something, young Loek?" Papa smiled and held out his hands. Part of the tradition was that the previous Watcher took charge of the frozen Firflake to carry it safely back to the field where Kristoff waited. Loek's face slightly blushed, as Papa let the Firflake slide across the open air until it was floated just above Loek's upturned palms. Nicholas smiled and winked, and Loek beamed with pride. He moved slowly towards the trees, his face squinched with concentration and his tongue sticking out between his lips as he tried to find just the right position for the Firflake to balance above his hands.

In a moment or less, the two men were the only ones on the shore of the brook. Papa stayed staring at the sky a little longer, watching the first snowfall of the year begin.

"Well, old friend." Nicholas spoke after a moment. "We've a lot to do this year—a whole world to visit, between your children and mine. Are you ready?"

"Hello, old friend." Papa Knecht embraced Nicholas, patting him on the small of his back. "Yes. Let's begin."

Acknowledgments

I wanted to write a Christmas story that I could eventually read to my nephew and niece. I think I succeeded. It would not exist if not for the feedback, critiques and support of the many people who have read and listened to it over the years.

And so, heartfelt thanks go to:

My family, whose unending support as I've continually found new fields to challenge myself in has kept me sane and grounded: my late parents Rosemary and Raymond Cardno, who got to read a very early version of this before my mother passed away; my amazingly supportive sister Lorraine, and her kids Vincent (Buddy) and Renee (Squirmy Worm) Bostjancic; my aunt and uncle, Nancy and Ed Frey, who continue to host Christmas Eve dinners and keep our family traditions alive; my cousins Lauren, Tim, Kaylee and Michael Miliambro; my god-parents Nan Cannon and John and Ginger Morganti who have always been there for me; my aunt Terry Cornelia who believed in my writing before there was any substantial writing to believe in; and all the Cardnos, LaPintas, Bessemers, Diazes, Bukowskis, Frugis', Cornelias, Hellers, Freys, Miliambros, Comittos and Hajkowskis.

The Cornues, for being a second family and providing quiet (and sometimes not so quiet) places to write, rewrite, contemplate and procrastinate. Special thanks to Jon for being a fantastic sounding board for rewrites, to Don for his amazing artwork, and to Ben for the author photo that accompanied the original edition.

My small army of honorary nieces and nephews across the U.S., Canada, and Australia , who always make me want to be a better writer, and a better man, than I usually am.

My hometown's influence on the stories I tell and the way I tell them is undeniable: thanks to the "old guard" of Mahopac. I honed my craft in the theater and English departments of my alma mater: the "Elmira College Literary and Theatrics Society" (you know who you are!) kept (and continue to keep) me from being too serious. I have been blessed with several "homes away from home" as I travel the country: my thanks to all the extended family and friends who take me in when I'm on the road for work. I've been a member of STAPA, the Super-Team Amateur Press Alliance since 1983: I owe thanks to my fellow comic book geeks for pushing me to write more and better. I've been blogging for a few years now and am thankful to all of my on-line friends and fellow authors for their insight and encouragement.

For mentoring me in the art and craft of Storytelling I have to thank Brian "Fox" Ellis.

And for bringing The Firflake back into print in

this special new illustrated edition, my thanks to Bryan Thomas Schmidt (who also gave me my first semi-professional and professional short story sales; thank you for championing my work), Guy Anthony De Marco over at PublicationEngineering.com for the beautiful interior design work, A.R. Redington for the wonderful new cover design, and Boralis Books.

Thanks For Reading

Neil Gaiman's poem "Nicholas Was…" inspired me to start writing my own holiday poem every year. The poem that leads off this slim volume came about 10 years into that sequence, after the early drafts of this book had been written. But it really all started with Neil.

Reviews are a writer's life-blood. If you enjoyed this book, please consider leaving a review on Goodreads, Amazon or wherever.

To find out more about my writing and song-writing, please visit www.anthonycardno.com. You can also find me on Twitter @talekyn.

About the Author

Anthony R. Cardno writes in hotel rooms and coffee shops more often than he writes at home in northwest NJ, so it's no wonder so many of his stories are about travelers. His stories have appeared in *Chiral Mad 4*, *Galactic Games*, *Kepler's Cowboys*, *One Thousand Words for War*, *Robbed Of Sleep Volume 4*, *Space Battles: Full Throttle Space Tales Volume 6*, *Beyond The Sun*, *OOMPH: A Little Super Goes A Long Way*, *Re-Launch*, *Tales of the Shadowmen Volume 10*, and in audio form on the StarShipSofa podcast. You can find him on Twitter @talekyn, on his blog at www.anthonycardno.com, and find his music on www.anthonycardno.bandcamp.com.